MUPPET BABIES'
Classic Children's Tales

CONTENTS

◆ ◆ ◆

Snow White and the Seven Dwarfs, by the Brothers Grimm

Treasure Island, by Robert Louis Stevenson

The Jungle Book, by Rudyard Kipling

Hans Brinker, or The Silver Skates, by Mary Mapes Dodge

Robin Hood, by Paul Creswick

Alice's Adventures in Wonderland, by Lewis Carroll

Pinocchio, by Carlo Collodi

Hansel and Gretel, by the Brothers Grimm

The Wizard of Oz, by L. Frank Baum

King Arthur and His Knights, retold by Sidney Lanier

Heidi, by Johanna Spyri

Peter Pan, by J. M. Barrie

INTRODUCTION

◆ ◆ ◆

Many of us have a very special children's book in our pasts; some of us even remember exactly when we encountered a favorite for the first time. Mine was *Alice in Wonderland,* which I first saw when I was nine, one rainy afternoon in a neighbor's attic. Yours might be *Peter Pan,* or *Treasure Island,* or *Heidi,* or *The Wizard of Oz.* We found some of these books on library shelves; some came to us in gift wrapping. Others were read to us by patient parents, who answered our endless questions. But all of them delighted us and enriched our lives.

Inspired by twelve imaginative photographs featuring the Muppet Babies and by exquisite border illustrations, the stories in this book are retellings of some episodes from the wonderful stories of our childhoods. They are meant to introduce young children to some of our favorite classic tales and to whet their appetites for the originals.

I was particularly happy to be involved in this project because, as I look back on my own childhood, my only regret about reading *Alice in Wonderland* when I did was that someone hadn't told me about it sooner!

—L. G.

SNOW WHITE
AND THE SEVEN DWARFS

Once a lovely little girl named Snow White was born to a joyful king and queen. Happiness would have reigned forever in the castle, but the queen soon died, and the king married a beautiful but heartless woman.

The new queen was really a witch, who owned a mirror that would always speak the truth. Day after day, she asked:

"Mirror, mirror, on the wall,
Who is fairest of them all?"

For years, the mirror answered:

"From the mountains to the sea,
There is none so fair as thee."

And the beautiful queen smiled. Then one day, the mirror replied.

"You are very fair, it's true,
But Snow White is lovelier far than you."

The queen was enraged. Immediately, she called a servant and commanded him to take the girl into the woods and kill her. But the servant took pity on Snow White, and he left her in the forest instead.

Snow White wandered through the forest for a long time. Finally, she came to a little house with seven little beds and seven places at the table. Then the owners came home. They were seven kindly dwarfs!

Snow White stayed with the dwarfs and was very happy in the forest. But the wicked queen soon learned from her magic mirror that Snow White was not dead. Disguised as an old woman, the queen went to the house of the seven dwarfs and tricked Snow White into eating a poisoned apple.

Snow White fell to the ground, and later the dwarfs saw what had happened. Weeping, they made a glass coffin for the beautiful Snow White and set it in the woods where they could visit it often.

One day, a handsome prince rode through the forest and saw the glass coffin. He fell in love with Snow White at first sight. The dwarfs agreed to let him take Snow White to his castle.

When the prince moved Snow White's coffin, the piece of poisoned apple fell from Snow White's throat, and she came to life once again. The overjoyed prince took Snow White home and made her his bride. The wicked queen died of anger when she found out. And the seven dwarfs rejoiced that Snow White was alive and happy once again.

TREASURE ISLAND

Jim Hawkins was a young lad whose father and mother owned an inn called the Admiral Benbow. One night, a gruff old pirate died at the inn. In the room where he lay, Jim and his mother found his sea chest. Jim opened it, and there he found a treasure map.

The map had once belonged to one of the bloodthirstiest pirates who ever lived, and he had once buried a fabulous treasure on Treasure Island.

Jim showed the map to his friend, Mr. Trelawny. They decided to hire a crew and go in search of the pirate's gold.

Mr. Trelawny was a man who trusted people too easily, and he hired a crew that was full of dishonest men. One of the worst of the men in the crew was a man with a wooden leg—Long John Silver.

Silver acted like an honorable friend, with his cheerful face and pet parrot. In fact, he was a sneaky pirate. His plan was to steal the gold once it had been found on Treasure Island.

Luckily, Jim Hawkins discovered Silver's plan. One night as he hid in a barrel of apples, Jim heard Silver boasting of his plans to his wicked friends in the crew.

When they reached the island, Jim met a strange, thin old man in raggedy clothes. With a wild voice, he said, "My name is Ben Gunn, lad. I was left here all alone on this island three years ago—marooned, I was."

Ben agreed to join up with Jim and his friends.

Long John Silver and his fellow pirates found the place where the treasure had been buried. They dug for hours in the hot sun, eager to get the gold. The treasure was nowhere to be found!

Silver roared at the hole they had dug. "No treasure!" he cried.

He was wrong. The treasure was still on Treasure Island, but it ended up in good hands. Jim's adventure was over, and he had the gold. Old Ben Gunn was finally able to leave the island and go home.

And they never saw Long John Silver again.

THE JUNGLE BOOK

There are many stories told in the jungle, but the most famous is the story of the boy who was raised by wolves.

It was a warm evening when Father Wolf awoke from a daylong nap in his cave. Mother Wolf lay nearby with her four cubs. As Father Wolf prepared to go hunting, a jackal came to the cave and said, "Take care! The Tiger, Shere Khan, has come to hunt on your hunting grounds!"

Father Wolf growled, "By the Law of the Jungle, he has no right to hunt here!"

Just then, they all heard the frightening sound of Shere Khan.

"Hush," said Mother Wolf. "Shere Khan is hunting Man. The Law of the Jungle forbids every beast to hunt Man."

The wolves heard a loud roar, and Father Wolf ran into the jungle to rescue the tiger's prey. "A child!" he cried, when he saw what the tiger was hunting.

Father Wolf picked up the child and carried him to the cave. There, Mother Wolf let him snuggle with her four cubs.

With a leap, Shere Khan appeared at the door of the cave. "Give me the child!" he roared.

Mother Wolf jumped up to protect her cubs. As she faced Shere Khan, their eyes glittered in the darkness. The tiger knew he could not win a fight against Mother Wolf in the cave. He walked away, saying that someday he would capture the child and eat him.

Mother Wolf decided to keep the child. Because he did not have fur like the wolves, Mother Wolf named the child Mowgli, which means *little frog*.

For Mowgli to live with the animals, the Law of the Jungle said two more animals must agree to care for him.

One night the leader of the wolves asked, "Who will speak for Mowgli?"

The first to speak was not a wolf, but Baloo, the sleepy brown bear. "I will teach Mowgli the Law of the Jungle," Baloo promised.

The second to speak for Mowgli was the panther named Bagheera. He convinced all the wolves to accept Mowgli because he knew that one day Mowgli would be able to defeat their enemy, the tiger, Shere Khan.

And that is how Mowgli entered the wolf pack and met his two best friends, Baloo and Bagheera.

HANS BRINKER, OR THE SILVER SKATES

In Holland, when the winds grow cold and winter comes, the waterways freeze over. Then you can see a very special sight: all the Dutch children, and the grown-ups too, skating to school and to work on the country's many canals turned to ice.

If you had been there many years ago, you might have seen Hans Brinker and his little sister, Gretel, on their rough wooden skates. Hans had made these skates because the family was too poor to afford real ones, for their father was very sick. He had been hurt years before in a fall, so Mrs. Brinker had to keep her family from starving—making a living from spinning, knitting, and raising vegetables.

Though Hans and Gretel wore home-made wooden skates, they were two of the best skaters in their village. One day, a contest was announced, and the prizes were to be two beautiful pairs of silver skates to the boy and girl who won. Hans and Gretel wanted very much to take part.

Hilda van Gleck, a kind girl from a wealthy family, saw how much they wanted to try their luck. She had only enough money of her own to pay for one pair of skates, but she eagerly gave Hans the money. Hans decided to buy skates for Gretel so that she could race in the contest.

Hans would not accept the money as a gift, so Hilda asked him to carve her a pretty wooden chain for her neck, just like the one he had carved for Gretel. The chain came out so well that after carving one, he carved another. In this way, he managed to save enough money to buy skates for both Gretel and himself.

Hans was excited about the contest, but his father's illness worried him. While going to purchase the skates, he caught sight of a very famous doctor. He begged the doctor to come to the aid of his father. The doctor kindly agreed, and soon, after an operation, Hans and Gretel's father began to get well.

And who were the winners of the contest? Gretel was the fastest skater among the girls and won her silver skates. Hans himself did not win the prize. But he did win the respect of all who knew him and the health of his father—which were greater prizes by far.

ROBIN HOOD

Many years ago, when good King Henry the Second and Queen Eleanor ruled England, a forest named Sherwood near the town of Nottingham was set aside for the king's hunting. No one except the king could kill a deer in Sherwood Forest.

Robin Fitzooth grew up near Sherwood. Robin, his cousin Will, and their friend Marian played happily there in the clear air beneath the green trees.

When Robin was a young man, the sheriff of Nottingham announced that there would be an archery contest. Robin decided to go to Nottingham to try for the prize. Then, as he was walking through the forest, he came upon some of the king's foresters.

"You plan to compete in an archery contest with those toy arrows?" laughed one.

"They are not toys," Robin angrily replied. "I will show you!" And without thinking, he pulled out his bow, took an arrow from his quill, and shot the best deer in a nearby herd.

"Do you know what you have done?" shouted the forester. "You have killed one of the king's deer. By the laws of our land, you are an outlaw!"

"Catch him!" shouted another. But Robin had grown up in the forest, and none knew it as well as he. He easily avoided his pursuers, and from that day on, he lived as an outlaw in Sherwood Forest.

In Sherwood, Robin met with other men who had been labeled outlaws—men who were not liked by the sheriff of Nottingham. They were merry, though, and they spent their time robbing from the rich and greedy friends of the sheriff, then giving their gold and silver pieces to the poor. Most people came to love Robin and his outlaw friends. But the sheriff of Nottingham was filled with anger.

The sheriff was determined to capture the young outlaw. So he decided to trick him. He announced another archery contest, with a golden arrow as the prize. He knew that Robin would surely come to compete, and when he did, the sheriff could easily arrest him.

But Robin carefully disguised himself in an old hood and cloak, completely fooling the sheriff, and won the golden arrow. Because of his disguise, he was known ever after as Rob in the Hood—or Robin Hood!

ALICE'S ADVENTURES IN WONDERLAND

Alice was a perfectly ordinary little girl. But one day, a very extraordinary thing happened to her. She was dozing on a riverbank when she happened to see a rabbit rush by. The odd thing was, he was wearing a waistcoat. And not only that— the rabbit then pulled a watch out of his pocket and cried, "Oh, dear! I shall be late!"

Alice decided to follow the rabbit and see where he was going. She followed him down a rabbit hole. The next thing she knew, she was in a strange land, where she had a number of curious adventures.

She soon discovered the house of the March Hare. In front of the house, a table was set out on the lawn. There, the March Hare, the Mad Hatter, and the Dormouse were having tea. The table was large, but the Hare, the Hatter, and the Dormouse were all crowded at one end.

"No room! No room!" they shouted when they saw Alice approach.

"There's plenty of room!" Alice replied with a frown. She sat down at the other end of the table and poured a cup of tea.

The March Hare and the Mad Hatter were telling riddles, and Alice thought this might be fun. But the riddles that were being told at this tea party were very odd, indeed.

"Why is a raven like a writing desk?" asked the Mad Hatter. "I believe I can guess that," Alice replied. She thought and she thought, but she simply couldn't figure out the answer. And when she finally asked him what the answer was, he told her, "There is no answer, none at all!"

The tea party got stranger and stranger. And the March Hare and the Mad Hatter were terribly rude to Alice. When she finally got up from the table and walked away, neither the Hatter nor the Hare paid any attention. The Dormouse fell instantly asleep. Alice almost hoped that they'd call her back, but they didn't. They were busy trying to stuff the Dormouse into the teapot.

Alice shook her head. "I'll never go *there* again," she declared. "That was the stupidest party I've ever seen in my life."

PINOCCHIO

Once upon a time, a wood-carver named Geppetto decided to make a puppet. He went to his good friend Antonio, who gave him a piece of wood. But it was a very unusual piece of wood.

Geppetto named his puppet Pinocchio. The first things Geppetto carved were Pinocchio's eyes. Geppetto was startled, indeed, when the eyes blinked! Then he carved a nose that sniffed, and a mouth that could talk. When he carved the little puppet's arms and legs, the puppet kicked him in the nose—and then ran away!

Geppetto raced after Pinocchio, calling to him to return. But Pinocchio, being a very naughty puppet, didn't listen, for Geppetto had forgotten to carve his ears. All through the town, Geppetto raced after his runaway puppet but he caused such a disturbance that Geppetto was arrested and thrown into jail. It was very unfair, for he wanted to be a good, kind father to Pinocchio.

After Geppetto was set free, Pinocchio continued running away. Each time, he had an amazing adventure. On one of these adventures, he met a beautiful fairy with blue hair.

Pinocchio told the fairy three lies, and each time he lied, his nose grew longer. Finally, it was so long that he could not move. When he tried to turn around, his nose bumped into the wall or the floor. The fairy only laughed.

"Why are you laughing at me?" Pinocchio wailed.

"I am laughing at the lies you have told." she replied.

"How do you know I have told you lies?" the puppet wanted to know.

"There are two kinds of lies, and they are always found out," she said. "Some lies have short legs, and some have long noses. Your lies are the kind that have long noses."

To teach Pinocchio a lesson, the fairy let him cry awhile. Then she called a flock of woodpeckers. They pecked at his nose until it was down to its normal size once again.

Finally, after many naughty adventures, Pinocchio learned to be good. He no longer broke poor Geppetto's heart, and was turned into a real live boy. The kindly old wood-carver then became the happiest father in the world.

HANSEL AND GRETEL

Hansel and Gretel lived with their father and stepmother in a little house in the woods. The family was so poor that they had hardly any food.

"Tomorrow, we must take the children deep into the forest and leave them," their stepmother told their father one night. "That way, at least we two will live." Their father refused at first, but his wife nagged him until he agreed.

But Hansel and Gretel heard what they were saying. That same night, Hansel crept outside and filled his pockets with white pebbles. The next day, as they were being led into the woods, the little boy dropped the pebbles along the path. When the moon came out, the children followed the pebbles home, and their father took them back in.

After a while, when food was scarce again, their stepmother persuaded their father to leave the children in the woods once more. This time, the door was barred, and Hansel could not collect pebbles as before. Instead, as they walked through the woods. Hansel crumbled bits of bread and dropped them on the path.

That night, in the moonlight, the children looked for the bread crumbs, but the birds had eaten them!

Tired and hungry, the children came to a cottage made entirely out of cakes and candies. They began eating the cottage, and a voice came from inside. It was a wicked witch, who liked nothing better than to eat children for supper.

The witch threw Hansel into the stable and forced Gretel to work for her. Hansel ate well, for the witch was fattening him up to eat. "Are you plump yet?" she would cry. "Stick out your finger so I can see." Since the witch couldn't see very well, Hansel held out an old bone and fooled her into thinking he was still too thin.

The witch then decided she would eat Gretel instead. She tried to trick the little girl into crawling into the oven to be cooked, but Gretel was more clever still.

"How can I fit in there?" Gretel asked. The witch crawled in to show her how. Gretel slammed the door shut, and the children were free!

After a long journey, the children found their home again. Their stepmother had gone, and their father was overjoyed to see them. From that day on the three lived happily in their cottage in the woods.

THE WIZARD OF OZ

Dorothy lived with her Aunt Em and Uncle Henry in Kansas. Her best friend was a little black dog named Toto.

One day, a tornado blew over Kansas. Before Dorothy could hide in the cellar with her aunt and uncle, the winds whisked up her house and blew it far, far away. When the house came down again, Dorothy found herself in the mysterious Land of Oz. The people in Oz were friendly and wanted to help Dorothy find her way back home.

"Follow the yellow brick road to the City of Emeralds," a good witch told her. "A great Wizard lives there. If anyone can tell you how to get back to Kansas, he can."

So Dorothy and Toto set off on their journey. They hadn't traveled far when they met a scarecrow. In Kansas, scarecrows were just scarecrows, but in Oz, they could talk! After Dorothy freed him from his perch, the Scarecrow asked if he could go with her to Oz.

"My head is stuffed with straw, but I want a real brain," he said. He felt sure that the great Wizard could give him one.

Dorothy liked the Scarecrow and agreed that they should travel together.

The yellow brick road led them into a forest. Dorothy and the Scarecrow heard a deep groan. They followed the sound until they came upon a Tin Woodman standing in one place completely unable to move. Dorothy and the Scarecrow oiled the Tin Woodman's joints so he could move again. When they told him where they were going, the Tin Woodman said, "Oh, let me go with you. I want to ask the Wizard for a heart."

They all set off. As the forest became darker and scarier, a great Lion bounded onto the yellow brick road and knocked down the Scarecrow and the Tin Woodman. When the Lion growled at Toto, Dorothy slapped him on the nose. The Lion began to cry. "I really don't have any courage," he wailed. So he asked if he could go with them to ask the Wizard to give him courage.

The Scarecrow, the Tin Woodman, the Lion, Dorothy, and Toto—in search of a brain, a heart, courage, and the way back to Kansas—headed for the Emerald City to find the Wizard of Oz.

KING ARTHUR

Long, long ago, a king named Uther Pendragon reigned in fair England. With the help of a great magician named Merlin, Uther ruled wisely and fairly all his life.

Merlin could see into the future, and he knew that Uther's only child, a boy named Arthur, would be in great danger. So, to protect the throne, Merlin secretly took the boy and gave him to the valiant knight Sir Ector. Sir Ector raised Arthur as his own son.

Years later, it came to pass that enemies of England attacked the country and poisoned good King Uther. On his deathbed, Uther declared that it was Arthur who was his rightful heir. But none of his lords had heard of Arthur, and not one was willing to yield the throne to a boy. So the lords began to fight among themselves to decide who would be king.

When Merlin saw this, he caused a great stone to appear in a churchyard in London. Embedded in the stone was a mighty sword. On the sword were these words in gold: WHOSOEVER CAN PULL THE SWORD FROM THE STONE WILL BE THE RIGHTFUL KING OF ENGLAND. On that day and for days thereafter, many tried to pull the sword from the stone, but no one could move it.

Some time later, a great tournament was held in London. Sir Ector, his son, Sir Kay, and Arthur went to take part.

When Sir Kay realized that he had left his sword at home, he commanded Arthur to go back and fetch it. Arthur remembered having seen the sword in the stone. He knew nothing about the magic of the sword, and so he decided to get *that* sword for Sir Kay.

Arthur went to the churchyard, easily pulled the sword from the stone, and brought it to Sir Kay. When Sir Ector saw the sword, he immediately recognized it. At first, Sir Kay claimed to have removed it from the stone, but Sir Ector finally discovered the truth. Only Arthur could pull the great sword from the stone.

The sword was put in the stone again, and Arthur pulled it out before all the lords of the land. Then they knew the truth: Arthur was the rightful king of England.

HEIDI

If you had been visiting the little Swiss town of Dorfli one sunny June morning many years ago, you would have seen a strange sight. There, beginning the long, steep climb up the mountain, was a five-year-old girl called Heidi and her Aunt Dete. Even though the sun was shining strongly, the little girl was dressed in all the clothes she owned, with her red scarf wound round and round her neck.

Heidi was getting hot, climbing up and up in all those clothes. Still, she cheerfully made her way up the mountain behind her aunt.

Dete had dressed Heidi this way so that she did not have to carry the child's few belongings. She was planning to leave Heidi with her grandfather, for Heidi's parents had died years before, and Dete no longer wanted to take care of her.

On the way, Heidi met Peter and his herd of goats. They were enjoying the warm sun and looked so comfortable that Heidi decided to take off several layers of her clothing. She wanted to be as carefree as the goats playing on the mountainside.

She left her clothes in a neat little pile. Then she and Dete kept climbing, Dete scolding her all the way, until they finally reached the grandfather's hut.

Heidi's grandfather was known in Dorfli as a stern and angry man. He had little interest in Heidi, but he cared nothing for the selfish Dete, who was so willing to abandon her niece. Grumpily, he agreed to keep Heidi. That day, as he watched the little girl happily exploring her new home, his angry feelings began to melt, like the snow on the mountaintops.

The very next day, Heidi joined young Peter, and together they climbed up to the fields where the goats grazed. As she romped in the fields of golden flowers, Heidi could hardly believe the beauty around her. She had never been so happy in all her life as she was in the glowing sunshine on the mountainside, playing among the gentle goats.

PETER PAN

All children grow up, except for Peter Pan. The day he was born, Peter decided he never, ever wanted to grow up. So he ran away to the Neverland—a magical island where children have exciting adventures.

Peter lived there for years and years. No matter how long it was, Peter was always a little boy. He even lost count of the years, for he could only count to three.

The Neverland itself was a lush, green island with caves and lagoons. The surrounding sea was ruled by pirates in a mighty ship. Peter's friends there were called the Lost Boys. They would have been perfectly happy, except for one thing. There were no stories in the Neverland because there were no mothers to tell them. Now and then, Peter and a fairy named Tinker Bell would fly away to the big city. There, he would sit on the windowsills of houses where he could listen to bedtime stories.

One of the houses that Peter visited belonged to the Darling family. Mrs. Darling told the most wonderful stories to her three children—Wendy, John, and Michael. Peter listened so hard that one night Mrs. Darling surprised him at the windowsill. Peter managed to escape, but he left his shadow. The next night, when he came back for it, he woke up Wendy.

Talking to Wendy, Peter discovered that she knew all of Mrs. Darling's stories. He invited her to the Neverland to tell them to the Lost Boys and to be their mother. Of course, John and Michael were invited, too.

"How do we get to the Neverland?" Wendy wanted to know.

"We fly!" Peter replied.

"But we can't fly!" John protested.

"Of course you can!" said Peter. "Just think wonderful, happy thoughts, and you'll float up like a balloon."

The children tried and tried, but even their loveliest thoughts didn't lift them an inch off the ground. Peter laughed.

"I almost forgot the most important part," he told them. "I'll just sprinkle some fairy dust on you—and away we'll go!"

The next thing they knew, the children were flying out the nursery window. They headed for the second star on the right and straight on till morning. They were on their way to many thrilling adventures in the Neverland.

BIBLIOGRAPHY

◆ ◆ ◆

Favorite Tales from Grimm, retold by Nancy Garden. Illustrated by Mercer Mayer. New York: Four Winds Press, 1982.

Treasure Island, by Robert Louis Stevenson. Illustrated by N. C. Wyeth. New York: Charles Scribner's Sons, 1911.

The Jungle Book, by Rudyard Kipling. Illustrated by Fritz Eichenberg. New York: Grosset & Dunlap Junior Library, 1950.

Hans Brinker, or The Silver Skates, by Mary Mapes Dodge. Illustrated by Cyrus Leroy Baldridge. New York: Grosset & Dunlap Junior Library, 1945.

Robin Hood, by Paul Creswick. Illustrated by N. C. Wyeth. New York: Charles Scribner's Sons, 1917.

Alice's Adventures in Wonderland and *Through the Looking-Glass*, by Lewis Carroll. Illustrated by Sir John Tenniel. New York: Dial Books for Young Readers, 1980.

Pinocchio, by Carlo Collodi. Translated by E. Harden. Illustrated by Roberto Innocenti. New York: Random House, 1988.

The Wonderful Wizard of Oz, by L. Frank Baum. Illustrated by W. W. Denslow. New York: William Morrow & Co./Books of Wonder, 1987.

The Boys' King Arthur, retold by Sidney Lanier, from Mallory's *Morte Darthur*. Illustrated by N. C. Wyeth. New York: Charles Scribner's Sons, 1917.

Heidi, by Johanna Spyri. Translated by Helen Dole. Illustrated by William Sharp. New York: Grosset & Dunlap Junior Library, 1945.

Peter Pan, by J. M. Barrie. Illustrated by Trina Schart Hyman. New York: Charles Scribner's Sons, 1980.